KENNETH GRAHAME

The Wind in the Willows

(Abridgment)

Illustrated by DICK CUFFARI

GROSSET & DUNLAP • Publishers • NEW YORK

CONTENTS

Abridgment

Library of Congress Catalog Card Number: 70-187515

ISBN: 0-448-02439-X

The River Bank

THE MOLE had been working hard all morning, spring-cleaning his home. Suddenly he flung down his brush and bolted out of the house without even waiting to put on his coat. Something up above was calling him, and he made for the steep little tunnel which led to the sun and air. He scraped and scratched, working busily with his little paws, till at last, *pop!* his snout came out into the sunlight, and he found himself rolling in the warm grass of a great meadow.

"This is fine!" he said to himself. "This is better than whitewashing!" Jumping off all his four legs at once, in the joy of living and the delight of spring without its cleaning, he made his way across the meadow.

He thought his happiness was complete when, as he meandered along, suddenly he stood by the edge of a river. Never in his life had he seen a river before—all glints and gleams and sparkles, rustle and swirl, chatter and bubble. The Mole was bewitched, entranced, fascinated.

As he sat on the grass and looked across the river, a dark hole in the bank opposite, just above the water's edge, caught his eye. As he gazed, something bright and small seemed to twinkle down in the heart of it, vanished, then twinkled once more like a tiny star. Then, as he looked, it winked at him, and so declared itself to be an eye; and a small face began gradually to grow up around it, like a frame around a picture. A brown little face, with whiskers.

It was the Water Rat!

Then the two animals stood and looked at each other cautiously.

"Hullo, Mole!" said the Water Rat.

"Hullo, Rat!" said the Mole.

"Would you like to come over?" inquired the Rat. He stooped and unfastened a rope and hauled on it; then lightly stepped into a little boat painted blue outside and white within, and just the size for two animals.

The Rat sculled smartly across and made fast. Then he held up his forepaw as the Mole stepped gingerly down. "Lean on that!" he said. Then the Mole, to his surprise and rapture, found himself actually seated in the stern of a real boat.

Waggling his toes from sheer happiness, he spread his chest with a sigh of contentment, and leaned back blissfully into the soft cushions. "*What* a day I'm having!" he said. "Let us start at once!"

The Rat pointed to a fat, wicker luncheon basket. "Shove that under your feet," he said to the Mole. "It's what I always take along on these trips."

The Mole, absorbed in the new life he was entering upon, the sparkle, the ripple, the scents and the sounds and the sunlight, trailed a paw in the water and dreamed long waking dreams. The Water Rat, like the good little fellow he was, sculled steadily on and did not disturb him.

"I beg your pardon," said the Mole, pulling himself together at last. "You must think me very rude; but all this is so new to me. So—this—is—a—River!"

"Yes," said the Rat. "It's my world, and I don't want any other. What it hasn't got is not worth having, and what it doesn't know is not worth knowing. Whether in winter or summer, spring or autumn, it's always got its fun and its excitements. Of course, it isn't what it used to be. Otters, kingfishers, dabchicks, moorhens, all of them about all day long and always wanting you to *do* something—as if a fellow had no business of his own to attend to!"

3

The Rat brought the boat alongside the bank, made it fast, helped the still awkward Mole safely ashore, and swung out the luncheon basket.

The Mole begged as a favor to be allowed to unpack it all by himself; and the Rat was very pleased to sprawl out on the grass and rest, while his excited friend shook out the tablecloth and spread it, took out all the mysterious packets one by one and arranged their contents, gasping, "Oh my! Oh my!" each time. When all was ready, the Rat said, "Now, pitch in, old fellow!" and the Mole was very glad to obey.

A broad glistening muzzle suddenly showed itself above the edge of the bank, and the Otter came out and shook water from his coat.

"Greedy beggars!" he observed, glancing at the food. "Why didn't you invite me, Ratty?"

"This was an impromptu affair," explained the Rat. "By the way—my friend, Mr. Mole."

"Proud, I'm sure," said the Otter, and the two animals were friends at once.

"Such a rumpus everywhere!" continued the Otter. "All the world seems out on the river today. Toad's out, for one, in his brand-new wager-boat. New togs, new everything!"

"Once, it was nothing but sailing," said the Rat. "Then he tired of that and took to punting. Nothing would please him but to punt all day and every day, and a nice mess he made of it. Last year it was houseboating, and we all had to go and stay with him in his houseboat, and pretend we liked it."

A stray May fly swerved unsteadily across the current near the surface. A swirl of water and a "cloop!" and the May fly was visible no more.

Neither was the Otter.

The Rat hummed a tune, and the Mole recollected that animal etiquette forbade any sort of comment on the sudden disappearance of one's friends at any moment, for any reason or no reason whatever.

"Well, well," said the Rat, "I suppose we ought to be moving. I wonder which of us had better pack the luncheon basket?" He did not speak as if he was eager to do so.

"Oh, please let me," said the Mole. So, of course, the Rat let him.

The afternoon sun was getting low as the Rat sculled gently homeward in a dreamy mood, murmuring poetry-things over to himself, and not paying much attention to Mole. But the Mole was very full of lunch, and self-satisfaction, and pride, and already quite at home in a boat (so he thought) and was getting restless, besides. He said, "Ratty! Please, _I_ want to row now!"

The Rat shook his head with a smile. "Not yet, my young friend," he said. "Wait till you've had a few lessons. It's not so easy as it looks. I really think you had better come and stop with me for a little time. I'll teach you to row, and to swim, and you'll soon be as handy on the water as any of us."

The Mole was so touched by this kind manner of speaking that he could find no voice to answer him; and he had to brush away a tear or two with the back of his paw.

When they got home, the Rat made a bright fire in the parlor, and planted the Mole in an armchair in front of it, having fetched down a dressing gown and slippers for him, and told him river stories till suppertime.

Supper was a cheerful meal; but very shortly a terribly sleepy Mole had to be led upstairs to the best bedroom, where he soon laid his head on his pillow in great peace and contentment, knowing that his new-found friend the River was lapping the sill of his window.

The Open Road

"RATTY," SAID the Mole suddenly, one bright summer morning, "if you please, I want to ask you a favor."

The Rat was sitting on the river bank, singing a little song which he had just made up about his friends the ducks, which he called:

DUCKS' DITTY

All along the backwater,
Through the rushes tall,
Ducks are a-dabbling,
Up tails all!

Ducks' tails, drakes' tails,
Yellow feet a-quiver,
Yellow bills all out of sight
Busy in the river!

Slushy green undergrowth
Where the roach swim—
Here we keep our larder,
Cool and full and dim.

Everyone for what he likes!
We like to be
Heads down, tails up,
Dabbling free!

High in the blue above
Swifts whirl and call—
We are down a-dabbling,
Up tails all!

"I don't know that I think so *very* much of that little song, Rat," observed the Mole cautiously. "But what I wanted to ask you was, won't you take me to call on Mr. Toad? I've heard so much about him."

"Why, certainly," said the good-natured Rat, jumping to his feet. "Get the boat out, and we'll paddle up there at once."

"He must be a very nice animal," observed the Mole, as he got in the boat and took the sculls, while the Rat settled himself comfortably in the stern.

"He is indeed the best of animals," replied Rat. "So simple, so good-natured, and so affectionate. Perhaps he's not very clever, but he has other good qualities."

Rounding a bend in the river, they saw a handsome, dignified old house of mellowed red brick, with well-kept lawns reaching down to the water's edge.

"There's Toad Hall," said the Rat. "Toad is rather rich, you know, and this is really one of the nicest houses in these parts."

They glided up the creek, disembarked, and strolled across the gay flower-decked lawns in search of Toad, whom they soon found sitting in a wicker garden chair, a large map spread out on his knees.

"Hooray!" he cried, jumping up on seeing them. "This is splendid!" He shook the paws of both of them warmly, never waiting for an introduction to the Mole. "You don't know how lucky it is, your turning up just now!"

"It's about your rowing, I suppose," said the Rat, with an innocent air.

"Oh, pooh! Boating!" interrupted the Toad. "Silly boyish amusement. I've given that up *long* ago. Sheer waste of time, that's what it is. No, I've discovered the real thing, the only genuine occupation for a lifetime. Come with me, dear Ratty, and your amiable friend also, if he will be so good."

He led the way to the stableyard, the Rat following with a mistrustful expression, and there they saw a gypsy caravan, shining with newness, painted yellow, with red wheels.

"There you are!" cried the Toad. "There's real life for you, right in that little cart. The open road, the dusty highway, the hedgerows! Camps, villages, towns, cities! Here today, and off tomorrow! Travel, change, interest, excitement! The whole world before you, and a horizon that's always changing! And this is the very finest cart of its sort that was ever built. Come inside and look at the arrangements. Planned 'em all myself, I did!"

It was indeed very compact and comfortable. Little sleeping bunks—a table that folded up against the wall—a cooking-stove, lockers, bookshelves, a birdcage with a bird in it; and pots, pans, and kettles of every size.

"All complete!" said the Toad triumphantly, pulling open a locker. "You see—biscuits, potted lobster, sardines—everything you can possibly want. Soda water, letter paper, bacon, jam, cards and dominoes. You'll find," he continued, as they descended the steps again, "that nothing whatever has been forgotten, when we make our start this afternoon."

"I beg your pardon," said the Rat slowly, as he chewed a straw, "but did I overhear you say something about '*we*' and '*start*' and '*this afternoon*'?"

"Now, don't begin talking in that stiff and sniffy way, because you know you've *got* to come," said Toad. "I can't possibly manage without you, so please consider it settled, and don't argue. You surely don't mean to stick to your dull old river all your life, and just live in a hole in a bank, and *boat*? I want to show you the world! I'm going to make an *animal* of you, my boy!"

During luncheon—which was excellent, of course, as everything at Toad Hall always was—the Toad painted the prospects of the trip and the joys of the open road in glowing colors. Somehow, it soon seemed taken for granted by all three of them that the trip was a settled thing.

When they were quite ready, the Toad led his companions to the paddock. An old gray horse was harnessed, and they set off, all talking at once. It was a golden afternoon. The smell of the dust they kicked up was rich and satisfying. Birds called and whistled to them cheerily. Good-natured wayfarers passing them gave them "Good day," or stopped to say nice things about their beautiful cart. And rabbits, sitting at their front doors in the hedgerows, held up their forepaws, and said, "Oh my! Oh my! Oh my!"

Late in the evening, tired and happy and miles from home, they turned the horse loose to graze, and ate a simple supper sitting by the side of the cart, while stars grew fuller and larger all around them. At last they turned into their little bunks in the cart. And Toad, kicking out his legs, sleepily said, "Well, good night, fellows! This is the real life for a gentleman!"

They had a pleasant ramble next day over grassy downs and along narrow by-lanes, and it was not till the afternoon that they came out on their first highroad.

They were moving along easily, when far behind them they heard a faint

warning hum, like the drone of a distant bee. Glancing back, they saw a small cloud of dust advancing on them at incredible speed, while from out the dust a faint "Poop-poop!" wailed like an uneasy animal in pain. In an instant the peaceful scene was changed, and with a blast of wind and a whirl of sound that made them jump, it was on them! The magnificent motorcar, immense, breath-snatching, passionate, with its pilot tense and hugging his wheel, flung an enveloping cloud of dust that blinded and enwrapped them, then dwindled to a speck in the far distance, changed back into a droning bee once more.

The old gray horse simply abandoned himself to his natural emotions. Rearing, plunging, he drove the cart backward toward the deep ditch at the side of the road. It wavered an instant—then there was a heart-rending crash —and the yellow cart lay on its side in the ditch.

Toad sat straight down in the middle of the dusty road, his legs stretched out before him, and stared fixedly in the direction of the disappearing motorcar. He breathed short, his face wore a placid, satisfied expression, and at intervals he faintly murmured. "Poop-poop!"

The Rat shook him by the shoulder. "Are you coming to help us, Toad?" he demanded sternly.

"Glorious, stirring sight!" murmured Toad, never offering to move. "The poetry of motion! The *real* way to travel! The *only* way to travel! Villages skipped, towns and cities jumped—always somebody else's horizon! Oh bliss! Oh poop-poop! Oh my! Oh my!"

"What are we to do with him?" asked the Mole of the Water Rat.

"Nothing at all," replied the Rat firmly. "Because there is really nothing to be done. You see, I know him from old. When he has a new craze, it always takes him that way, in its first stage. He'll continue like that for days now, quite useless for all practical purposes. Never mind him. It's five or six miles to the nearest town, and we must walk it. The sooner we start the better."

"But what about Toad?" asked the Mole anxiously, as they set off together.

"Oh, *bother* Toad," said the Rat savagely. "I've done with him!"

They had not gone very far, however, when there was a pattering of feet behind them, and Toad caught them up and thrust a paw inside the elbow of each of them. "Oh, Ratty!" he gasped. "You can't think how obliged I am to you for consenting to come on this trip! I wouldn't have gone without you, and then I might never have seen that—that swan, that sunbeam, that thunderbolt! I might never have heard that entrancing sound, or smelled that bewitching smell! I owe it all to you, my best of friends!"

The Rat turned from him in despair. "You see?" he said to the Mole. "He's quite hopeless. I give it up—when we get to the town we'll go to the railway station, and with luck we may get a train there that'll get us back to River Bank tonight."

On reaching the town they went straight to the station. Eventually, a slow train having landed them not very far from Toad Hall, they got out their boat, sculled down the river home, and at a very late hour sat down to supper.

The following evening the Mole, who had risen late and taken things very easy all day, was sitting on the bank fishing, when the Rat, who had been looking up his friends and gossiping, came strolling along to find him. "Heard the news?" he said. "It's the talk of the river bank. Toad went up to town by an early train this morning. And he has ordered a large and very expensive motorcar."

The Wild Wood

THE MOLE had long wanted to make the acquaintance of the Badger. But whenever the Mole mentioned his wish to the Water Rat he always found himself put off. "It's all right," the Rat would say, "Badger'll turn up some day or other—he's always turning up—and then I'll introduce you."

The Mole had to be content with this. But the Badger never came along, and every day brought its amusements. It was not till summer was long over, and cold and frost and miry ways kept them much indoors, that Mole again thought of the solitary gray Badger, who lived his own life by himself.

One afternoon, when the Rat in his armchair before the fire was alternately dozing and trying over rhymes that wouldn't fit, the Mole decided to go out by himself and explore the Wild Wood, and perhaps meet Mr. Badger.

It was a cold still afternoon with a hard steely sky overhead, when he slipped out of the warm parlor into the open air, pushing on cheerfully.

There was nothing to alarm him at first. Twigs crackled under his feet, logs tripped him, but that was all fun, and exciting. It led him on, and he penetrated to where the light was less, and trees crouched nearer and nearer.

Then the faces began.

It was over his shoulder, and indistinctly, that he first thought he saw a little evil wedge-shaped face, looking out at him from a hole. When he turned, the thing had vanished.

He quickened his pace, telling himself not to begin imagining things, or there would be no end to it. Then suddenly, as if it had been so all the time, every hole, far and near, seemed to have a face, coming and going rapidly.

If he could only get away from the holes in the banks, he thought, there would be no more faces. He swung off the path and plunged into the wood.

Then the whistling began.

Very faint and shrill it was, and far behind him, when he first heard it; but somehow it made him hurry forward. Then, still very faint and shrill, it sounded far ahead of him, and made him hesitate and want to go back. They were up and alert and ready, evidently, whoever they were! And he—he was alone, and unarmed, and far from any help; and the night was closing in.

Then the pattering began.

He thought it was only falling leaves at first, so slight and delicate was the sound of it. Then the pattering increased till it sounded like sudden hail on the dry-leaf carpet spread around him. The whole wood seemed running now, running hard, hunting, chasing, closing in round something or—somebody? In panic, he began to run too, aimlessly. He ran up against things, he fell over things and into things, he darted under things and dodged round things. At last he crawled into the deep dark hollow of an old beech tree, which offered shelter, concealment—perhaps even safety. Anyhow, he was too tired to run any farther and could only snuggle down into some dry leaves. As he lay there panting and trembling, and listened to the whistlings and the patterings outside, he knew at last, in all its fullness, that dread thing which the Rat had tried to shield him from—the Terror of the Wild Wood!

Meantime the Rat, warm and comfortable, dozed by his fireside. Then a coal slipped, and he woke with a start.

"Moly!" he called several times, and, receiving no answer, got up and went out into the hall.

The Mole's cap was missing from its peg. His galoshes, which always lay by the umbrella stand, were also gone.

The Rat left the house and carefully examined the muddy surface of the ground outside, hoping to find the Mole's tracks. There they were, sure enough, leading direct to the Wild Wood.

The Rat stood in deep thought for a minute or two. Then he re-entered the house, strapped a belt around his waist, shoved two pistols into it, took up a stout cudgel, and quickly set off for the Wild Wood.

It was already almost dusk when he plunged without hesitation into the wood, looking anxiously for any sign of his friend, all the time calling out cheerfully, "Moly, Moly, Moly! Where are you? It's me—Rat!"

He had hunted through the wood for an hour or more, when at last he heard a little answering cry. Guiding himself by the sound, he made his way to the foot of an old beech tree, and from out of the hole in it came a feeble voice, saying, "Ratty! Is that really you?"

The Rat crept into the hollow, and there he found the Mole, exhausted and still trembling. "Oh, Rat!" he cried, "I've been so frightened!"

"Oh, I quite understand," said the Rat soothingly. "Now then, we really must pull ourselves together and make a start for home while there's still a little light left. It will never do to spend the night here, you understand."

"Why? What's up, Ratty?" asked the Mole.

"*Snow* is up," replied the Rat briefly, "or rather, *down*. It's snowing hard. We must make a start, and take our chance, I suppose. The worst of it is, I don't exactly know where we are. And now this snow makes everything look so very different."

It did indeed. The Mole would not have known that it was the same wood. However, they set out bravely, pretending that they recognized an old friend in every fresh tree that grimly and silently greeted them.

An hour or two later they sat down on a fallen tree trunk to recover their breath. They had fallen into several holes and got wet through; the snow was getting so deep that they could hardly drag their little legs through it, and the trees were thicker than ever. There seemed to be no end to this wood, and no beginning, and no difference in it, and, worst of all, no way out.

"We can't sit here very long," said the Rat. "We shall have to make another push for it, and do something or other. The cold is too awful for anything, and the snow will soon be too deep for us to wade through."

Once more they got on their feet, but suddenly the Mole tripped up and fell forward on his face with a squeal.

"Oh, my leg!" he cried. "Oh, my poor shin!" and he sat up on the snow and nursed his leg in both his front paws.

"Poor old Mole!" said the Rat kindly. "You don't seem to be having much luck today, do you? Let's have a look at the leg. Yes," he went on, going down on his knees to look, "you've cut your shin, sure enough. That was never done by a branch or a stump. Looks as if it was made by a sharp edge of some-thing in metal."

"Well, never mind what done it," said the Mole, forgetting his grammar in his pain. "It hurts just the same, whatever done it."

Some ten minutes' hard work, and the point of the Rat's cudgel struck something that sounded hollow. He worked till he could get a paw through and feel; then called to Mole to come and help him. Hard at it went the two animals, till at last the result of their labors was in full view.

In the side of what had seemed to be a snowbank stood a solid-looking little door, painted a dark green. An iron bellpull hung by the side, and below it, on a small brass plate, they could read by the aid of moonlight: MR. BADGER.

The Mole fell backward on the snow from sheer surprise and delight. "Rat," he cried, "you're a wonder! A real wonder, that's what you are!"

While the Rat attacked the door with his stick, the Mole sprang up at the bellpull, clutched it and swung there, both feet well off the ground, and from quite a long way off they could faintly hear a deep-toned bell.

They waited patiently for what seemed a very long time, stamping in the snow to keep their feet warm. At last they heard the sound of slow shuffling footsteps approaching the door from the inside.

There was the noise of a bolt shot back, and the door opened a few inches, enough to show a long snout and a pair of sleepy blinking eyes.

"Oh, Badger," cried the Rat, "let us in, please. It's me, Rat, and my friend Mole, and we've lost our way in the snow."

"What, Ratty, my dear little man!" exclaimed the Badger. "Come in, both of you, at once. Well, I never! Lost in the snow! And in the Wild Wood, too, and at this time of night! But come in with you."

The two animals tumbled over each other in their eagerness to get inside, and soon found themselves amid the warmth of a large fire-lit kitchen.

The kindly Badger thrust them down to toast themselves at the fire, and bade them remove their wet coats and boots. Then he fetched them dressing gowns and slippers, and himself bathed the Mole's shin with warm water and bandaged the cut till the whole thing was just as good as new, if not better.

When at last they were thoroughly toasted, the Badger called them to the table to dine. Conversation was impossible for a long time; and when it was slowly resumed, it was that regrettable sort of conversation that results from talking with your mouth full.

When supper was finished at last, and after they had chatted for a time about things in general, the Badger said heartily, "Now then! tell us the news from your part of the world. How's old Toad going on?"

"Oh, from bad to worse," said the Rat gravely. "Another smashup only last week, a bad one. But he's convinced he's a heaven-born driver, and nobody can teach him anything."

"How many has he had?" inquired the Badger gloomily.

"Smashes, or machines?" asked the Rat. "Oh, well, after all, it's the same thing—with Toad. This is the seventh."

"He's been in hospital three times," put in the Mole, "and as for the fines he's had to pay, it's simply awful to think of."

"Yes, and that's part of the trouble," continued the Rat, "Killed or ruined —it's got to be one of the two things, sooner or later. Badger! We're his friends—oughtn't we to do something?"

The Badger went through a bit of hard thinking. "Now, look here," he said at last, rather severely, "of course you know I can't do anything *now*?"

His two friends assented, quite understanding his point. No animal, according to the rules of animal etiquette, is ever expected to do anything strenuous, or heroic, or even moderately active during the winter. All are sleepy—some actually asleep.

"Very well, then!" continued the Badger. "*But,* when once the year has really turned, and the nights are shorter, we'll take Toad seriously in hand. We'll stand no nonsense whatever. We'll bring him back to reason. We'll *make* him be a sensible Toad."

Homecoming

THE MOLE and the Water Rat, in high spirits, were returning across country after a long day's outing with Otter, hunting and exploring on the wide uplands where streams had their first small beginnings; and the shades of the short winter day were closing in on them.

They plodded along steadily, each of them thinking his own thoughts. The Mole's ran a good deal on supper, as it was pitch-dark, and it was all a strange country to him as far as he knew, and he was following obediently in the wake of the Rat, leaving the guidance entirely to him. As for the Rat, he was walking a little way ahead, his shoulders humped, his eyes fixed on the road in front of him; so he did not notice when one of these mysterious fairy calls from out the void suddenly reached Mole in the darkness, making him tingle through and through. He stopped dead in his tracks, his nose searching hither and thither in its efforts to recapture something.

Home! That was what they meant, those caressing appeals, those soft touches wafted through the air, those invisible little hands pulling and tugging, all one way! Why, it must be quite close by him at that moment, his old home that he had hurriedly forsaken and never sought again, that day when he first found the river! And now, with a rush of old memories, how clearly it stood up before him, in the darkness! Shabby indeed, and small and poorly furnished, and yet his, the home he had made for himself, the home he had been so happy to get back to after his day's work. And the home had been happy with him, too, evidently, and was missing him, and was telling him so, through his nose, reminding him that it was there, and wanted him.

The call was clear, the summons was plain. He must obey it instantly, and go. "Ratty," he called, full of joyful excitement, "hold on! Come back! I want you, quick!"

"Mole, we mustn't stop now, really!" the Rat called back. "We'll come for it tomorrow, whatever it is you've found. But I daren't stop now—it's late, and the snow's coming on again, and I'm not sure of the way! And I want your nose, Mole, so come on quick, there's a good fellow!" And the Rat pressed forward on his way without waiting for an answer.

Poor Mole stood alone in the road, his heart torn apart, and a big sob gathering, gathering, somewhere low down inside him. Up and up, it forced its way to the air, and then another, and another, and others thick and fast; till poor Mole at last gave up the struggle, and cried freely and helplessly and openly, now that he knew it was all over and he had lost what he could hardly be said to have found.

The Rat, astonished and dismayed at the Mole's grief, did not dare to speak for a while. At last he said, very quietly and sympathetically, "What is it, old fellow? Whatever can be the matter?"

Poor Mole found it difficult to get any words out. "I know it's a—shabby, dingy little place," he sobbed forth at last, brokenly: "not like—your cozy quarters—or Toad's beautiful hall—or Badger's great house—but it was my own little home—and I was fond of it—and I went away and forgot all about it—and then I smelled it suddenly—on the road, when I called and everything came back to me with a rush—and I *wanted* it!—Oh dear! Oh dear!"

Recollection brought fresh waves of sorrow, and sobs again took full charge of him, preventing further speech.

The Rat stared straight in front of him, saying nothing, only patting Mole gently on the shoulder. He waited till Mole's sobs became gradually less stormy. Then he rose from his seat, and, remarking carelessly, "Well, now we'd really better be getting on, old chap!" set off up the road again, over the way they had come.

"Wherever are you (hic) going to (hic), Ratty?" cried the tearful Mole, looking up in alarm.

"We're going to find that home of yours, old fellow," replied the Rat pleasantly, "so you had better come along, for it will take some finding, and we shall want your nose."

Mole stood a moment rigid, while his uplifted nose, quivering slightly, felt the air.

Then a short, quick run forward—a fault—a check—a try back; and then a slow, steady, confident advance.

The Rat, much excited, kept close to his heels as the Mole, with something of the air of a sleepwalker, crossed a dry ditch, scrambled through a hedge, and nosed his way over an open field.

Suddenly, without giving warning, he dived; but the Rat was on the alert, and promptly followed him down the tunnel to which his unerring nose had faithfully led him.

It was close and airless, and the earthy smell was strong, and it seemed a long time to Rat before the passage ended and he could stand erect and stretch and shake himself. The Mole struck a match, and by its light the Rat saw that they were standing in an open space neatly swept and sanded underfoot, and directly facing them was Mole's little front door, with "Mole End" painted over the bellpull at the side.

Mole reached down a lantern from a nail on the wall and lit it, and he hurried Rat through the door, lit a lamp in the hall, and took one glance around his old home. He saw the dust lying thick on everything, saw the cheerless, deserted look of the long-neglected house, and its worn and shabby contents—and collapsed again on a hall chair. "Oh, Ratty!" he cried dismally, "why ever did I bring you to this poor, cold little place, on a night like this, when you might have been at River Bank by this time, with all your own nice things about you!"

The Rat, however, was running here and there, opening doors, inspecting rooms and cupboards, and lighting lamps and candles. "What a capital little house this is!" he called out cheerily. "So compact! So well planned! Everything here and everything in its place! We'll make a jolly night of it. The first thing we want is a good fire; I'll fetch the wood and the coals, and you get a duster, Mole, and try and smarten things up a bit."

Encouraged by his companion, the Mole roused himself and dusted and polished, while the Rat, running to and fro with armfuls of fuel, soon had a cheerful blaze roaring. He hailed the Mole to come and warm himself; but suddenly sounds were heard from the forecourt—sounds like the scuffling of small feet in the gravel and a confused murmur of tiny voices.

"What's up?" inquired the Rat, pausing in his labors.

"I think it must be the field mice," replied the Mole, with a touch of pride in his manner. "They go round carol-singing regularly at this time of the year. They're quite an institution in these parts."

"Let's have a look at them!" cried the Rat, jumping up and running to the door to fling it open.

In the forecourt, lit by the dim rays of a lantern, some eight or ten little

field mice stood in a semicircle, red scarfs around their throats, their fore-paws thrust deep into their pockets, their feet jiggling for warmth. With bright beady eyes they glanced shyly at each other, sniggering a little, sniffing and applying coat sleeves a good deal. As the door opened, one of the elder ones that carried the lantern was just saying, "Now then, one, two, three!" and forthwith their shrill little voices sang an old-time carol.

"Very well sung, boys!" cried the Rat heartily. "And now come along in, all of you, and warm yourselves by the fire."

"Oh, Ratty!" cried the Mole in despair, plumping down on a seat, with tears impending. "We have nothing to give them!"

"You leave all that to me," said the masterful Rat. "Here, you with the lantern! Come over this way. Tell me, are there any shops open at this hour of the night?"

"Why, certainly, sir," replied the field mouse respectfully. "At this time of the year our shops keep open to all sorts of hours."

"Then look here! said the Rat. "You go off at once, and you get me—"

Here much muttered conversation ensued. Finally, there was a chink of coin passing from paw to paw, the field mouse was provided with a basket for his purchases, and off he hurried. The rest of the field mice gave them-selves up to enjoyment of the fire.

Soon the field mouse with the lantern reappeared, staggering under the weight of his basket. Under the generalship of Rat, everybody was set to do something or to fetch something. In a very few minutes supper was ready, and Mole took his place at the head of the table, thinking what a happy home-coming this had turned out, after all.

Mr. Toad

It was a bright morning in the early part of summer. The Mole and the Water Rat were finishing breakfast in their little parlor, when a heavy knock sounded at the door.

The Badger strode heavily into the room, and stood looking at the two animals with an expression full of seriousness. The Rat let his egg spoon fall on the tablecloth, and sat openmouthed.

"The hour has come!" said the Badger at last with great solemnity.

"What hour?" asked the Rat uneasily, glancing at the clock.

"*Whose* hour, you should say," replied the Badger. "Why, Toad's hour! I said I would take him in hand as soon as the winter was well over, and I'm going to take him in hand today!"

"Toad's hour, of course!" cried the Mole delightedly, "I remember now! *We'll* teach him to be a sensible Toad!"

"This very morning," continued the Badger, taking an armchair, "another new and exceptionally powerful motorcar will arrive at Toad Hall on approval or return. We must be up and doing, before it is too late. Off to Toad Hall! The work of rescue shall be accomplished."

"Right you are!" cried the Rat. "We'll rescue the poor unhappy animal! We'll convert him! He'll be the most converted Toad that ever was before we've done with him!"

They set off up the road, Badger leading the way, and reached the carriage drive of Toad Hall to find, as the Badger had anticipated, a shiny new motorcar, painted a bright red (Toad's favorite color), in front of the house. As they neared the door, it was flung open, and Mr. Toad, in goggles, cap, gaiters, and enormous overcoat, came swaggering down the steps, drawing on his gloves.

"Hullo! Come on, you fellows!" he cried cheerfully on catching sight of them. "You're just in time to come with me for a jolly—to come for a jolly—for a—er—jolly—"

His words faltered and fell away as he noticed the stern unbending look on the faces of his silent friends.

The Badger strode up the steps. "Take him inside," he said sternly to his companions. Then, as Toad was hustled through the door struggling and protesting, he turned to the chauffeur in charge of the new motorcar.

"I'm afraid you won't be wanted today," he said. "Mr. Toad has changed his mind. He will not require the car. Please understand that this is final. You needn't wait." Then he followed the others inside and shut the door.

"Now, then!" he said to the Toad, when the four of them stood together in the hall, "first of all, take those ridiculous things off!"

"Shan't!" replied Toad. "What is the meaning of this? I demand an instant explanation."

"Take them off him, then, you two," ordered the Badger briefly.

They had to lay Toad out on the floor, kicking and calling all sort of names, before they could get to work properly. Then the Rat sat on him, and the Mole got his motor clothes off him bit by bit, and they stood him up on his legs again.

"You knew it had to come to this, sooner or later, Toad," the Badger explained severely. "You've disregarded all the warnings we've given you,

you've gone on squandering the money your father left you, and you're getting us animals a bad name by your furious driving and your smashes. We never allow our friends to make fools of themselves beyond a certain limit; and that limit you've reached. Now, you're a good fellow in many respects, and I don't want to be too hard on you. I'll make one more effort to bring you to reason."

He took Toad firmly by the arm, led him into the smoking room, and closed the door behind them.

"*That's* no good!" said the Rat. "Talking to Toad'll never cure him. He'll *say* anything."

After some three-quarters of an hour the door opened, and the Badger reappeared, solemnly leading by the paw a very limp and dejected Toad. His skin hung baggily about him—and his legs wobbled.

"Sit down there, Toad," said the Badger kindly, pointing to a chair. "My friends," he went on, "I am pleased to inform you that Toad has at last seen the error of his ways. He is truly sorry for his misguided conduct in the past, and he has undertaken to give up motorcars entirely and forever. I have his solemn promise to that effect."

"That is very good news," said the Mole gravely.

"Very good news, indeed," observed the Rat, "if only—*if* only——"

There was a long, long pause. Toad looked desperately this way and that, while the other animals waited in grave silence. At last he spoke.

"No!" he said a little sullenly, but stoutly, "I'm *not* sorry. And it wasn't folly at all! It was simply glorious!"

"What?" cried the Badger, greatly scandalized. "You backsliding animal, didn't you tell me just now, in there—"

"Oh, yes, yes, in *there*," said Toad impatiently. "I'd have said anything in *there*. You're so moving, and so convincing, and put all your points so frightfully well—you can do what you like with me in *there*, and you know it. But I find that I'm not a bit sorry, really, so it's no earthly good saying I am; now, is it?"

"Then you don't promise," said the Badger, "never to touch a motorcar again?"

"Certainly not!" replied Toad emphatically. "On the contrary, I faithfully promise that the very first motorcar I see, poop-poop! Off I go in it!"

"Told you so, didn't I?" observed the Rat to the Mole.

"Very well, then," said the Badger firmly, rising to his feet. "I feared it would come to this all along. You've often asked us three to come and stay with you, Toad; well, now we're going to. Take him upstairs, you two, and lock him in his bedroom, while we arrange matters between ourselves."

"It's for your own good, Toady, you know," said the Rat kindly, as Toad, kicking and struggling, was hauled up the stairs. "Think what fun we shall have together, just as we used to, when you've quite got over this painful attack of yours!"

"We'll take great care of everything for you till you're well, Toad," said the Mole; "and we'll see your money isn't wasted, as it has been."

"No more incidents with the police, Toad," said the Rat, as they thrust him into his bedroom.

"And no more weeks in hospital," added the Mole, turning the key.

They descended the stair, Toad shouting abuse at them through the keyhole, and the three friends then met to discuss the situation.

"It's going to be a tedious business," said the Badger, sighing. "I've never

seen Toad so determined. However, we will see it out. We shall have to take turns to be with him, till the poison has worked itself out of his system."

They arranged watches accordingly. Each animal took it in turns to sleep in Toad's room at night, and they divided the day up between them.

One fine morning the Rat went upstairs to relieve Badger, whom he found fidgeting to be off and stretch his legs in a long ramble. "Toad's still in bed," he told the Rat, outside the door. "Now, you look out, Rat! When Toad's quiet and submissive, there's sure to be something up. I know him. Well, now I must be off."

"How are you today, old chap?" inquired the Rat cheerfully, as he approached Toad's bedside.

He had to wait some minutes for an answer. At last a feeble voice replied, "Thank you so much, dear Ratty! So good of you to inquire! But first tell me how you are yourself, and the excellent Mole?"

"Oh, *we're* all right," replied the Rat. "Mole," he added incautiously, "is going out for a run round with Badger. They'll be out till luncheontime, so I'll do my best to amuse you. Now jump up, there's a good fellow, and don't lie moping there."

"Dear, kind Rat," murmured Toad, "how very far I am from 'jumping up' now—if ever! But do not trouble about me. I hate being a burden to my friends, and I do not expect to be one much longer. Indeed, I almost hope not."

"Well, I hope not, too," said the Rat heartily. "You've been a fine bother to us all this time, and I'm glad to hear it's going to stop. It isn't the trouble we mind, but you're making us miss such an awful lot."

"I'm afraid it *is* the trouble you mind, though," replied the Toad languidly. "You're tired of bothering about me. I'm a nuisance, I know."

"You are, indeed," said the Rat. "But I tell you, I'd take any trouble on earth for you, if only you'd be a sensible animal."

"If I thought that, Ratty," murmured Toad, more feebly than ever, "then I would beg you—for the last time, probably—to fetch the doctor. But don't you bother. It's only a trouble, and perhaps we may as well let things take their course."

"Why, what do you want a doctor for?" inquired the Rat, coming closer and examining him. He certainly lay very still and flat, and his voice was weaker and his manner much changed.

"Surely you have notice of late—" murmured Toad. "But no—why should you? Noticing things is only a trouble. Tomorrow, indeed, you may be saying to yourself, 'Oh, if only I had noticed sooner! If only I had done something!' But no; it's a trouble. Never mind—forget that I asked."

"Look here, old man," said the Rat, beginning to get rather alarmed, "of course I'll fetch a doctor to you, if you really think you want him." He hurried from the room, not forgetting, however, to lock the door carefully behind him, and then ran off to the village on his errand of mercy.

The Toad, who had hopped lightly out of bed as soon as he heard the key turned in the lock, watched him eagerly from the window till he disappeared down the carriage drive. Then he dressed as quickly as possible, filled his pockets with cash which he took from a small drawer in the dressing table, and next, knotting the sheets from his bed together and tying one end fast, he scrambled out the window of his bedroom, slid lightly to the ground, and marched off, whistling a merry tune.

At first he took bypaths, and crossed many fields, and changed his course several times, in case of pursuit; but now, feeling safe, and the sun smiling brightly on him, he almost danced along the road in his satisfaction and conceit.

He strode along, his head in the air, till he reached a little town, where the sign of "The Red Lion" reminded him that he had not breakfasted that day. He marched into the inn and ordered the best luncheon that could be provided.

He was about halfway through his meal when a familiar sound drew nearer and nearer. The car turned into the inn yard, and Toad had to hold on to the leg of the table to conceal his excitement. Presently the party entered the room, hungry, talkative, and gay. Toad at last could stand it no longer. He slipped out of the room quietly, paid his bill, and moved outside to the inn yard. "There cannot be any harm," he said to himself, "in my only *looking* at it!"

The car stood in the middle of the yard, quite unattended. Toad walked slowly round it, inspecting, criticizing, musing deeply.

"I wonder," he said to himself presently, "I wonder if this sort of car *starts* easily?"

Next moment, hardly knowing how it came about, he found himself, somehow, seated in the driver's seat. As if in a dream, he drove the car round the yard and out through the archway. Then he increased his speed, and as the car moved forth on the highroad through the open country, he was only conscious that he was Toad once more, Toad at his best and highest, Toad the Lord of the lone trail, before whom all must give way.

❀   ❀   ❀   ❀   ❀

"To my mind," observed the Chairman of the Bench of Magistrates cheerfully, "the *only* difficulty that presents itself is, how we can possibly make it sufficiently hot for the ruffian whom we see cowering before us. Let me see: he has been found guilty, on the clearest evidence, first, of stealing a valuable motorcar; secondly, of driving to the public danger; and, thirdly, of gross impertinence to the police. Mr. Clerk, will you tell us, please, what penalty we can impose for each of those offenses? Without, of course, giving the prisoner the benefit of any doubt, because there isn't any."

The Clerk scratched his nose with his pen. "Judging by what we've heard from the witness box, even if you only believe one-tenth part of what you heard, and I never believe more myself—the penalties, if added together correctly, come to nineteen years—"

"First-rate!" said the Chairman.

"—So you had better make it a round twenty years and be on the safe side," concluded the Clerk.

"An excellent suggestion!" said the Chairman approvingly. "Prisoner! Pull yourself together and try and stand up straight. It's going to be twenty years for you this time. And mind, if you appear before us again, upon any charge whatever, we shall have to deal with you very seriously!"

The hapless Toad, loaded with chains, was dragged from the Courthouse, shrieking, praying, protesting; across the marketplace, past hooting school children; across the hollow-sounding drawbridge, under the frowning archway of the grim old castle; past guardrooms and sentries; up timeworn winding stairs; across courtyards, where mastiffs strained at their leash and pawed the air to get at him; on, past the rack-chamber and the thumbscrewroom, past the private scaffold, till they reached the door of the grimmest dungeon.

The rusty key creaked in the lock, the great door clanged shut; and Toad was a helpless prisoner in the stoutest castle in Merry England.

Toad's Adventures

WHEN TOAD found himself in this dank and noisome dungeon, he flung himself at full length on the floor, and shed bitter tears, and abandoned himself to dark despair. "This is the end of everything," he said. "Now I must languish in this dungeon, till people who were proud to say they knew me, have forgotten the very name of Toad! Oh, wise old Badger! Oh, clever, intelligent Rat and sensible Mole! What sound judgments, what a knowledge of men and matters you possess! Oh, unhappy and forsaken Toad!" With lamentations such as these he passed his days and nights for several weeks.

Now the jailer had a daughter who assisted her father in the lighter duties of his post. She was particularly fond of animals, and, pitying the misery of Toad, knocked one day at the door of Toad's cell.

"Now, cheer up, Toad," she said coaxingly, on entering, "and sit up and dry your eyes and be a sensible animal." She carried a tray, with a cup of fragrant tea steaming on it; and a plate with very hot buttered toast. The smell of that buttered toast simply talked to Toad; talked of warm kitchens, of breakfast on bright frosty mornings, of cozy parlor firesides on winter evenings, of the purring of contented cats, and the twitter of sleepy canaries. Toad sat up, dried his eyes, sipped his tea and munched his toast, and soon began talking freely about himself, and the house he lived in.

The jailer's daughter encouraged him to go on. "Tell me about Toad Hall," she said. "It sounds beautiful."

"Toad Hall," said the Toad proudly, "is a self-contained gentleman's residence, very unique; dating in part from the fourteenth century, but having every modern convenience. Up-to-date sanitation. Five minutes from church, post office, and golf links." Continuing, his spirits quite restored to their usual level, Toad told her about the boathouse, and the fishpond, and the old walled kitchen garden; and about the pigsties, and the stables, and the henhouse; and about the dairy, and the washhouse, and the china cupboards, and the banqueting hall, and the fun they had there when the other animals were gathered round the table. Then she wanted to know about his animal friends, and was very interested in all he had to tell her about them and how they lived. When she said good night, Toad was very much the same self-satisfied animal that he had been of old. He sang a little song or two, and then had an excellent night's rest and the pleasantest of dreams.

They had many interesting talks together, after that; and the jailer's daughter thought it a great shame that a poor little animal should be locked up in prison for what seemed to her a very trivial offense.

One morning the girl was very thoughtful. "Toad," she said presently, "just listen, please. I have an aunt who is a washerwoman; she does the washing for all the prisoners in this castle. Now, this is what occurs to me: you're very rich—at least you're always telling me so—and she's very poor. A few pounds wouldn't make any difference to you, and it would mean a lot to her. I think you could come to some arrangement by which she would let you have her dress and bonnet and so on, and you could escape from the castle as the official washerwoman."

"You are a good, kind, clever girl," said Toad. "Introduce me to your worthy aunt, if you will be so kind, and I have no doubt that the excellent lady and I will be able to arrange terms."

Next evening the girl ushered her aunt into Toad's cell, bearing his week's washing pinned up in a towel. In return for his cash, Toad received a cotton print gown, an apron, a shawl, and a rusty black bonnet. "Now, Toad," said the girl, "take off that coat and waistcoat of yours; you're fat enough as it is."

Shaking with laughter, she proceeded to "hook-and-eye" him into the cotton print gown, arranged the shawl, and tied the strings of the rusty bonnet under his chin.

"You're the very image of her," she giggled, "only I'm sure you never looked half so respectable in all your life before. Now, good-bye, Toad, and good luck. Go straight down the way you came up."

With a quaking heart, Toad set forth cautiously on what seemed to be a most harebrained and hazardous undertaking; but he was soon agreeably surprised to find how easy everything was. The washerwoman's squat figure in its familiar cotton print seemed a passport for every barred door and gateway.

At last he heard the wicket gate in the great outer door click behind him, felt the fresh air of the outer world upon his anxious brow, and knew that he was free!

He made his way to the railroad station, consulted a timetable, and found that a train, bound more or less in the direction of his home, was due to start in half an hour. "What luck!" said Toad, his spirits rising rapidly, and went to buy his ticket. But when he put his fingers, in search of the necessary money, where his waistcoat pocket should have been, he found—not only no money, but no pocket to hold it, and no waistcoat to hold the pocket! To his horror he recollected that he had left both coat and waistcoat behind him in his cell. In his misery he made one desperate effort to carry the thing off, and said, "Look here! I find I've left my purse behind. Just give me that ticket, will you, and I'll send the money on tomorrow. I'm known in these parts."

The clerk stared at him and then laughed. "I should think you were pretty well known in these parts," he said, "if you've tried this game often. Stand away from the window, please, madam."

Baffled and full of despair, he wandered blindly down the platform where the train was standing, and tears trickled down each side of his nose.

"Hullo, mother!" said the engine driver, "what's the trouble?"

"Oh, sir!" said Toad, crying afresh, "I am a poor unhappy washerwoman, and I've lost all my money, and can't pay for a ticket, and I *must* get home tonight somehow, and whatever I am to do I don't know. Oh dear! Oh dear!"

"Well, I'll tell you what I'll do," said the good engine driver. If you wash a few shirts for me when you get home, and send 'em along, I'll give you a ride on my engine. It's against regulations, but we're not so very particular in these out-of-the-way parts."

The Toad's misery turned into rapture as he eagerly scrambled up into the cab of the engine. Of course, he had never washed a shirt in his life, and couldn't if he tried, but he thought: "When I get safely home to Toad Hall, and have money again, I will send the engine driver enough to pay for a washing, and that will be the same thing, or better."

The train moved out of the station, and as the speed increased, the Toad could see on either side of him real fields and trees, and hedges, and cows, and horses. As he thought how every minute was bringing him nearer to Toad Hall, and sympathetic friends, and money to chink in his pocket, and a soft bed to sleep in, and good things to eat, he began to skip and shout and sing snatches of song, to the great astonishment of the engine driver.

They had covered many and many a mile when Toad noticed that the engine driver, with a puzzled expression on his face, was leaning over the side of the engine and listening hard. Then he saw him climb on to the coals and gaze out over the top of the train; then he returned and said to Toad: "It's very strange; we're the last train running in this direction tonight, yet it looks as if were being pursued!"

The miserable Toad, crouching in the coal dust, tried hard to think of something to do, with dismal want of success.

"They are gaining on us fast!" cried the engine driver. "And the engine is crowded with policemen and plainclothes detectives, waving revolvers and sticks; all waving, and shouting the same thing—'Stop, stop, stop!'"

Then Toad fell on his knees among the coals and, raising his clasped paws, cried, "Save me, dear kind Mr. Engine driver, and I will confess everything! I am not the simple washerwoman I seem to be! I am a toad—the well-known and popular Mr. Toad. I have just escaped, by daring and cleverness, from a dungeon, and if those fellows on that engine recapture me, it will be chains and bread and water and straw and *misery* once more for poor, unhappy, innocent Toad!"

The engine driver looked very grave and said, "I fear that you have been indeed a wicked toad, and by rights I ought to give you up to justice. But the sight of an animal in tears always makes me soft-hearted. So cheer up, Toad! I'll do my best, and we may beat them yet!"

They piled on more coals, shoveling furiously, and the train shot into a tunnel, and the engine rushed and roared and rattled, till at last they shot out at the other end into fresh air and saw a wood upon either side of the line. The driver shut off steam and put on brakes. Toad jumped, rolled down a short embankment, picked himself up unhurt, scrambled into the wood and hid.

Peeping out, he saw his train get up speed again and disappear. Then out of the tunnel burst the pursuing engine, roaring and whistling, her motley crew waving their weapons and shouting, "Stop! stop! stop!" When they were past, the Toad had a hearty laugh—for the first time since he was thrown into prison.

But he soon stopped laughing when he came to consider that it was now very late and dark and cold, and he was in an unknown wood, with no money and no chance of supper, and still far from friends and home. He dared not leave the shelter of the trees, so he struck into the wood and sought the safety of a hollow tree, where with branches and dead leaves he made himself as comfortable a bed as he could, and slept soundly till morning.

The front door of the hollow tree faced eastward, so Toad was called at an early hour; partly by the bright sunlight streaming in on him, partly by the coldness of his toes. Sitting up, he rubbed his eyes first and his complaining toes next, wondering for a moment where he was. He shook himself, combed the dry leaves out of his hair with his fingers, and marched forth into the comfortable morning sun, cold but confident, hungry but hopeful.

As he tramped along, he thought of his adventures and escapes, and how when things seemed at their worst he had always managed to find a way out. "Ho, ho!" he said to himself as he marched along with his chin in the air. "What a clever Toad I am! There is surely no animal equal to me for cleverness in the whole world!"

After some miles of country lanes he reached the highroad, and as he turned into it and glanced along its length, he saw approaching him a speck that turned into a dot and then into a blob, and then into something very familiar.

He stepped confidently out into the road to hail the motorcar, which came along at an easy pace, slowing down as it neared the lane; when suddenly he became very pale, his heart turned to water and his knees shook and yielded under him. The approaching car was the very one he had stolen out of the yard of the Red Lion Hotel on that fatal day when all his troubles began! He sank down in a shabby, miserable heap in the road, murmuring to himself in his despair, "It's all up! It's all over now! Chains and policemen again! Prison again! Dry bread and water again!"

The terrible motorcar drew slowly nearer and nearer, till at last he heard it stop just short of him. Two gentlemen got out and walked round the trembling heap lying in the road, and one of them said, "Oh dear! This is very sad! Here is a poor old thing—a washerwoman apparently—who has fainted in the road! Let us lift her into the car and take her to the nearest village, where doubtless she has friends."

They tenderly lifted Toad into the motorcar and propped him up with soft cushions, and proceeded on their way.

When Toad heard them talk in so kind and sympathetic a manner, and knew that he was not recognized, his courage began to revive, and he cautiously opened first one eye and then the other.

"Look!" said one of the gentlemen, "she is better already. The fresh air is doing her good. How do you feel now, ma'am?"

"Thank you kindly, sir," said Toad in a feeble voice, "I'm feeling a great deal better!"

Toad was almost himself again by now. He sat up, looked about him, and turned to the driver at his side.

"Please, sir," he said, "I wish you would kindly let me try and drive the car for a little. I've been watching you carefully, and it looks so easy and so interesting, and I should like to be able to tell my friends that once I had driven a motorcar!"

The driver laughed good-naturedly at the proposal, and said, to Toad's delight, "Bravo, ma'am! I like your spirit. Have a try!" Toad eagerly scrambled into the seat vacated by the driver, took the steering wheel in his hands, and set the car in motion, but very slowly and carefully at first.

Toad went a little faster; then faster still, and faster. He put on full speed. The rush of air in his face, the hum of the engine, and the light jump of the car beneath him intoxicated his brain. "Washerwoman, indeed!" he shouted recklessly. "Ho! ho! I am the Toad, the motorcar snatcher, the prison-breaker, the Toad who always escapes! Sit still, and you shall know what driving really is, for you are in the hands of the famous, the skillful, the entirely fearless Toad!"

With a cry of horror the whole party rose and flung themselves on him. "Seize him!" they cried. "Seize the Toad, the wicked animal who stole our motorcar! Bind him, chain him, drag him to the nearest police station! Down with the desperate and dangerous Toad!"

Alas! they should have thought, they should have remembered to stop the motorcar somehow before playing any pranks of that sort. With a half-turn of the wheel the Toad sent the car crashing through the low hedge that ran along the roadside. One mighty bound, a violent shock, and the wheels of the car were churning up the thick mud of a horsepond.

Toad found himself flying through the air and was just beginning to

wonder whether it would go on until he developed wings and turned into a Toad-bird, when he landed on his back in the soft rich grass of a meadow.

He picked himself up rapidly, and set off running across country as hard as he could, scrambling through hedges, jumping ditches, pounding across fields, till he was breathless and weary. Suddenly the earth failed under his feet, he grasped at the air, and found himself head over ears in deep water, rapid water, water that bore him along. He had run straight into the river!

He rose to the surface and tried to grasp the reeds and the rushes that grew along the water's edge close under the bank, but the stream was so strong that it tore them out of his hands. Presently he saw that he was approaching a big dark hole in the bank, just above his head, and as the stream bore him past, he reached up with a paw and caught hold of the edge and held on.

As he stared before him into the dark hole, some bright small thing shone and twinkled in its depths, moving toward him. A face grew up gradually around it, and it was a familiar face!

Brown and small with whiskers.

Grave and round, with neat ears and silky hair.

It was the Water Rat!

The Rat put out a neat little brown paw, gripped Toad firmly by the scruff of the neck, and gave a great hoist and a pull. The waterlogged Toad came up slowly over the edge of the hole, till at last he stood safe and sound in the hall, the water streaming off him, but happy to find himself once more in the house of a friend.

"Oh, Ratty!" he cried. "I've been through such times since I saw you last, you can't think! Such trials, such sufferings, and all so nobly borne! Then such escapes, such disguises, such subterfuges, and all so cleverly planned and carried out! Been in prison—got out of it, of course! Humbugged everybody —made 'em all do exactly what I wanted! Oh, I *am* a smart Toad, and no mistake!"

"Toad," said the Water Rat, gravely and firmly, "you go off upstairs at once, and take off that old cotton rag that looks as if it might formerly have belonged to some washerwoman, and clean yourself thoroughly, and put on some of my clothes and try and come down looking like a gentleman if you *can;* for a more shabby, bedraggled, disreputable-looking object than you are I never set eyes on in my whole life! Now, stop swaggering and arguing, and be off! I'll have something to say to you later!"

By the time Toad came down again, luncheon was on the table. While they ate, Toad told the Rat all his adventures, dwelling chiefly on his own cleverness, and presence of mind in emergencies.

When at last Toad had finished his tale, he said, "Now I'm going to stroll gently down to Toad Hall, and get into clothes of my own, and set things going again on the old lines. I've had enough of adventures. From now on, I shall lead a quiet, steady, respectable life."

✿　　✿　　✿　　✿　　✿

The four animals continued to lead their lives in great joy and contentment. Toad, after due consultation with his friends, selected a handsome gold chain and locket set with pearls, which he dispatched to the jailer's daughter with a letter that even the Badger admitted to be modest, grateful, and appreciative; and the engine driver, in his turn, was properly thanked and compensated for all his pains and trouble.